Walt Disney's
DONALD DUCK
and the
Witch Next Door

gb **GOLDEN PRESS**
Western Publishing Company, Inc.
Racine, Wisconsin

Sixth Printing, 1977

"Unca Donald, look!" called Huey Duck.

"Someone built a house on the vacant lot next door!" cried Dewey Duck.

"I think we're going to have a new neighbor," said Louie Duck.

Donald peeked over the fence. "By golly, you're right," he said. "But the house wasn't there yesterday. There was nothing on the lot last night. And what a funny-looking house! If I didn't know better, I'd say it was made out of gingerbread."

Dewey tasted a corner of the new house. "It *is* made out of gingerbread!" he said.

"A gingerbread house!" cried Louie. "Only witches live in gingerbread houses. I read that in one of my storybooks."

"Witches?" Donald Duck laughed and laughed. "There are no such things as witches."

The moment Donald said that, the door of the gingerbread house popped open. A lady with purple hair and big green eyes looked out. "Who doesn't believe in witches?" shouted the lady.

"I don't," Donald Duck answered.

"You will," said the lady. "My name is Madam Mim, and I built this house by magic."

"How?" asked Donald.

"Easy! I'm a witch!" She proved it by raising her hands and casting a spell.

POUFF! Donald turned into a watermelon!

The nephews' eyes opened wide. Huey, Dewey, and Louie saw what had happened, and they cried, "We believe in witches! We believe! We do! Please change that watermelon back into Unca Donald."

Madam Mim looked sly. "I want some cobwebs for my new house. We witches like cobwebs—they make a place cozy, you know. I'll trade you your uncle for some cobwebs."

"You bet!" the boys shouted together, and they ran home to find cobwebs.

Dewey gathered some in the garage and in the garden shed.

Louie looked in the lumber pile.

Huey searched the cellar.

They also swept some from the chandelier, the
attic, and the storeroom.

"Is that all?" asked Madam Mim when the boys brought her a basketful of cobwebs.

"It's all we have," Huey argued.

"Then I suppose it will have to do," said Madam Mim. She changed the watermelon back into Donald Duck and went inside to decorate her new house with the cobwebs.

"WAK!" sputtered Donald, looking dazed. "What happened? I felt all green and cold!"

"Our new neighbor *is* a witch," replied Huey. "She turned you into a watermelon."

"Hmmmm," said Donald. "If she's a witch, I wonder if she has a flying broom."

Before another day passed, they saw that Mim did indeed fly on a broom.

Donald said happily, "Doesn't that look like fun? I wonder if she'll let me borrow it now and then. After all, she *is* using our cobwebs."

"Don't ask, Unca Donald," warned Louie. "She might change you back into a watermelon—or maybe a cabbage or even a rutabaga."

So Donald Duck didn't ask Madam Mim for the
loan of her broomstick. Instead, he waited until she
was busy planting toadstools in her backyard. Then
he snatched the broom and flew away.

"Great leaping bat wings!" shouted Madam Mim
when she saw Donald on her broom.

Donald didn't know how to control the broom, and he was wobbling badly. But Mim knew all about brooms, and she was determined to teach Donald a lesson. She cast a spell, and the broom kicked like a wild mustang!

ZOOM! The broom flew up, up, up—right through a cloud.

"WAK!" squawked Donald Duck when he almost bumped into a passing eagle.

"Slow down! Slow down!" shouted Donald, but
the broom went even faster. It sped across the sky.
It raced with the starlings. It scattered the bluebirds,
and it broke up a formation of migrating geese.

"Easy! Easy!" pleaded Donald, but the broom didn't take it easy. It crashed through a high-flying kite. It played tag with a jetliner. It bucked and swerved and looped. It zigged and zagged and rolled —and it tossed Donald off.

Donald fell down, down, down until . . . BUMP!
He landed on a damp, soggy island in the middle of
Great Dismal Swamp. And who should be waiting
on that damp, soggy island? Why, Madam Mim was
waiting, of course.

The broom settled to the ground and leaned against
Madam Mim. "My poor broom!" said Madam Mim.
"It's so tired it can hardly stand up. I'll teach you a
lesson, you thieving duck!"

She changed Donald into a frog. "There!" she said.
"For all I care, you can stay here in the swamp forever." Then she got on her broom and flew home.

Donald didn't stay in the swamp forever. Madam Mim had forgotten that frogs can hop and frogs can swim. Donald hopped and swam and swam and hopped, until he was safe on dry ground.

"I'll never steal a broom again," said Donald to himself. "I'll never take anything!" Suddenly Donald wasn't a frog anymore. He was Donald Duck. He hurried right home as fast as his webbed feet could carry him.

"Drat!" said Madam Mim when she saw him. "He's back. Well, if he's going to live here, I'm not! But before I go, I'll give him back his cobwebs—and with interest!"

Madam Mim called her friends. They came from far and near and brought cobwebs, cobwebs, and cobwebs—and even a few spiders.

"WAK! What a mess!" yelled Donald. After he settled down, he told the boys, "Bring me a broom."

"Our broom doesn't fly," said Huey.

"Thank goodness!" said Donald, and he began to sweep up cobwebs and spiders.

The boys didn't stay to watch. They knew what
to do when a neighbor moves away and leaves a gingerbread house behind. They hurried over and ate
the gingerbread house, right down to the very last
gingerbread shingle!